Eva and Sadie and the Worst Haircut EVER!

By Jeff Cohen • Illustrated by Elanna Allen

Eva and Sadie and the Worst Haircut EVER!

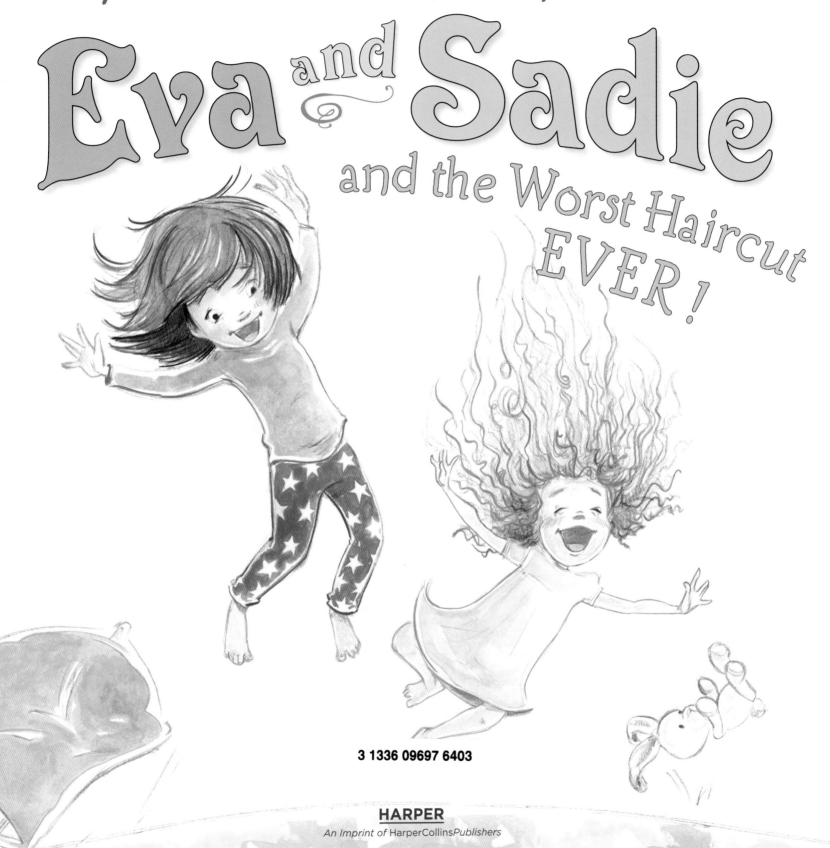

HARPER

An Imprint of HarperCollinsPublishers

For Eva, Sadie, and Izzi. You make everything better.
—J.C.

In memory of Annie Rooney
—E.A.

Eva and Sadie and the Worst Haircut EVER!
Text copyright © 2014 by Jeff Cohen
Illustrations copyright © 2014 by Elanna Allen
All rights reserved. Manufactured in China.
For information address HarperCollins Children's Books, a division of HarperCollins Publishers, 10 East 53rd Street, New York, NY 10022.
www.harpercollinschildrens.com
ISBN 978-0-06-224906-7
The artist used pencil, watercolor, and a touch of Adobe Photoshop to create the illustrations for this book.
Typography by Jeanne L. Hogle
14 15 16 17 18   SCP   10 9 8 7 6 5 4 3 2 1

First Edition

I'm Sadie, and this is *my* little sister, Eva.
Eva has long curly hair. I think it's too long,
too curly, and way too MUCH!

Her hair is so long, it almost goes down to her tush!
But no one has EVER cut Eva's hair.

It's so long that our mom
tries to make her pigtails,

ponytails,
and long, crazy braids.

Eva *never* wants to brush her hair.
I think she should. Her hair can get
out of control.

The only thing she does
like is our big basket of hair
stuff—sparkly clips, headbands,
ribbons, hair flowers, and shiny
barrettes.

One day, when Eva's braids are getting scraggly, I get an idea!

"Eva! Do you want to take your hair out of those braids? It would look more pretty!"

So I help her take out her braids.

That's when I get another idea.

"Do you want a haircut?"

I ask her.

"YES!!!!"

So I run to the bathroom.

I climb up onto the edge of the bathtub,
and I find our mom's scissors.

I climb back down and I get right to work.

First I cut off the curly parts.

Snip, snip, snip!

"Hmm. Some parts are short and some parts are long. I have to keep working."

Snip, snip, snip, snip, snip, snip!

When I am finished, I look down at the pile of hair on the floor, and that's when I know things have gone terribly wrong.

Uh-oh, I think. This is bad, *bad, bad!*

But Eva *likes* it.

So she runs downstairs to
show our mom and dad.
I stay *right* where I am.

"Look at my haircut, Mommy," I can hear Eva saying. "Isn't it nice?"

Our mom and dad are usually pretty calm.
But sometimes they lose their cool.

This time . . .

. . . they *definitely* lose their cool.

I *knew* my parents weren't going to like Eva's haircut.
So I grab the hair and hide it under the radiator.
Then I pile up books and
stuffed animals all around
so no one can find it.

But Eva tells them that *I* cut her hair,
which doesn't *make* me happy.

When Dad comes upstairs, I show him the
pile of hair and tell him what happened.
"I guess I shouldn't have cut Eva's hair,"
I say. "I feel really, really terrible.

"But that kind of stuff happens a few times in everybody's life, right?

"Or maybe just once is enough."

"That's right," he says. "Just once. Now you know not to do it again."

My parents say I have to have a consequence for what I did. So I can't eat *my* favorite chocolate candy for a week. I guess that makes sense. They said they learned a lesson, too. They're putting the scissors where I can't find them.

"Since that's settled, let's go get Eva a *real* haircut," Dad says. "And this time, *she* gets to decide how to cut it."

And that's what we do.

After the *real* haircut, I show Eva all the cool things she can do with her new short hair.
After all, I am the big sister.

And the funny thing is . . . now that Eva's hair is short,
we can't imagine it any other way.